Bugtown BOOGiE

by Warren Hanson
paintings by Steve Johnson & Lou Fancher

LAURA GERINGER BOOKS
An Imprint of HarperCollinsPublishers

Bugtown Boogie

Text copyright © 2008 by Warren Hanson

Illustrations copyright © 2008 by Steve Johnson and Lou Fancher

Manufactured in China.

For information address HarperCollins Children's Books, a division of HarperCollins Publishers,
1350 Avenue of the Americas, New York, NY 10019.
www.harpercollinschildrens.com

Library of Congress Cataloging-in-Publication Data

Hanson, Warren.

Bugtown Boogie / by Warren Hanson ; illustrated by Steve Johnson and Lou Fancher. — 1st ed.

p.   cm.

Summary: While strolling home through the woods one evening, a young boy happens upon a rollicking dancing party in Bugtown.

ISBN-10: 0-06-059937-5 (trade bdg.) — ISBN-13: 978-0-06-059937-9 (trade bdg.)

ISBN-10: 0-06-059938-3 (lib. bdg.) — ISBN-13: 978-0-06-059938-6 (lib. bdg.)

[1. Insects—Fiction. 2. Parties—Fiction. 3. Dance—Fiction. 4. Stories in rhyme.] I. Johnson, Steve, date, ill. II. Fancher, Lou, ill. III. Title.

PZ8.3.H19655Bug 2008   2006029207

[E]—dc22   CIP

                                                                                                                      AC

Typography by Lou Fancher

1 2 3 4 5 6 7 8 9 10
❖

To Patty, my Ladybug
—W.H.

To Warren
—S.J. & L.F.

I was strollin' on home through the woods the other night,
When I saw something a-flashin'—it was shinin' mighty bright!
It was blinkin' and a-winkin' near the bottom of a tree,
So I scurried on over just to see what I could see.

What I saw there in that tree trunk
Where it met the forest floor
Was a million little lights around a teeny tiny door.
I got down upon my knees so I could take a look inside,
And what I found before me made my eyes pop open wide!

It was a Bugtown Boogie.
Buzz-a-ruzz-a-buzz-a-ruzz,
A Bugtown Boogie.
Grick grack. Grick grack.
A Bugtown Boogie, shakin' up the woods tonight.

There were bugs of every color, every shape, and every size.
They had legs and wings and stingers and a million little eyes.

Some of them were fuzzy,

and some were in a shell,

But they all had come to party, just as far as I could tell.

They were all in there a-dancin' to a buggie-wuggie beat,
Swingin' and a-wingin' and a-tappin' all their feet.
They were buzzin' by the dozen, swarmin' all around the floor.
And when I blinked my eyes, it seemed like there were even more!!

At the Bugtown Boogie.
Freega. Freega.
The Bugtown Boogie.
Zmmm. Zmmm.
The Bugtown Boogie,
shakin' up the woods tonight.

Out there in the middle was a colony of Ants,
And they were shakin' their behinds
Like they had people in their pants!
Black Ants. Red Ants. I never saw so many.
I'll bet there were about a million-thousand-hundred-twenty!

When the Centipedes were dancin', they took up a lot of space,
'Cause their feet, they were a-flyin' up and down and every place.
As the music was explodin' like the powder in a keg,
Those Centipedes were shimmyin' and shakin' every leg.

Down at the Bugtown Boogie.

Froppit! Froppit!

The Bugtown Boogie.

Orp. Snorp.

The Bugtown Boogie, shakin' up the woods tonight.

The Humbug drummed with a stick in every hand,
And he banged a buggy beat for everybody in the band.

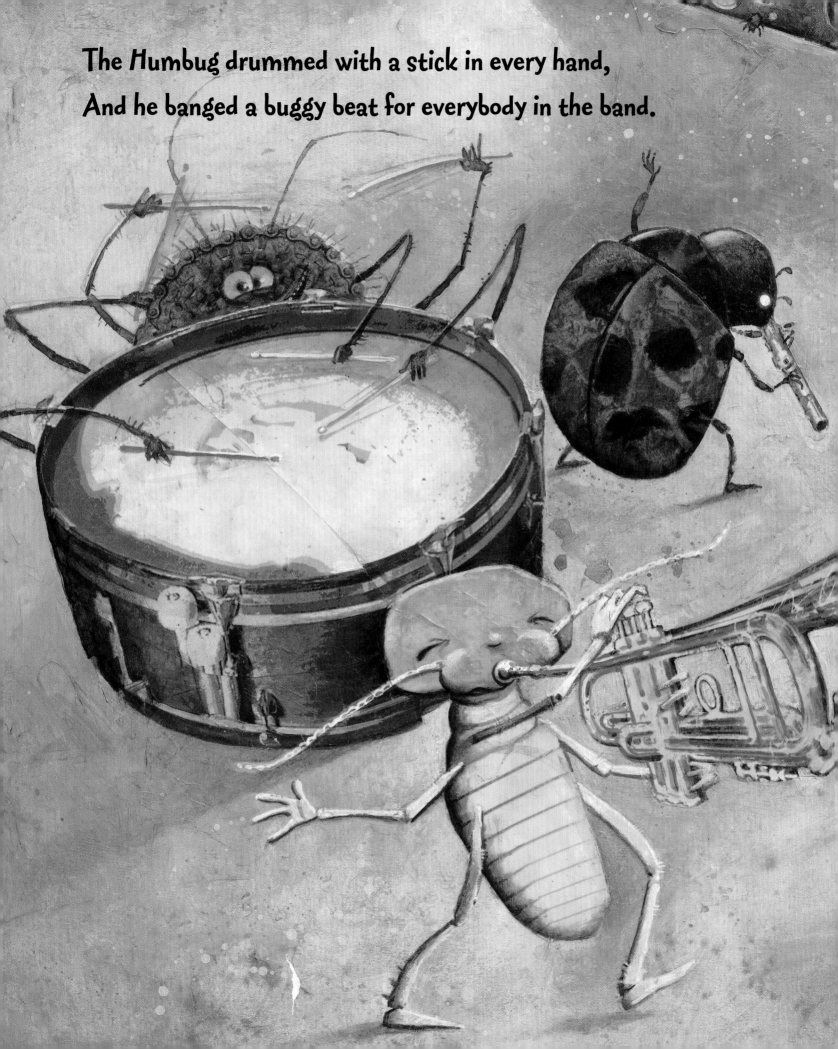

The Termite on the trumpet played a TAT-a-TAT-a-TOOT,
While the Ladybug was groovin' on her tiny little flute.

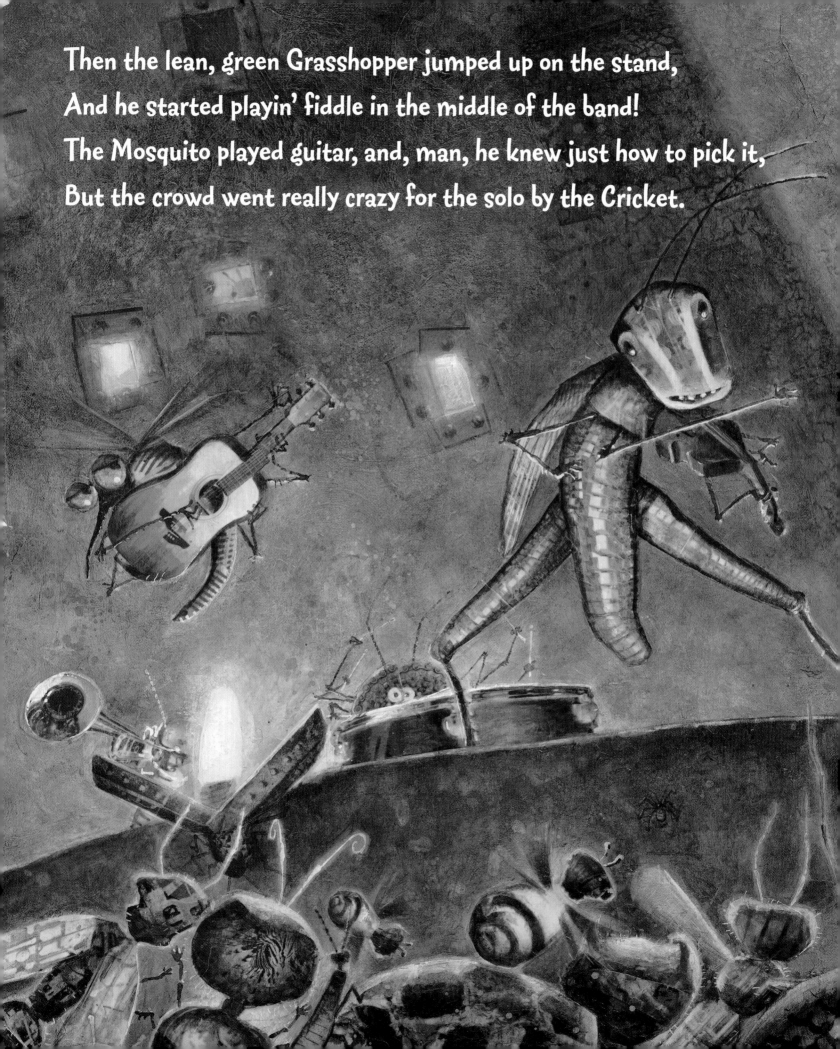

Then the lean, green Grasshopper jumped up on the stand,
And he started playin' fiddle in the middle of the band!
The Mosquito played guitar, and, man, he knew just how to pick it,
But the crowd went really crazy for the solo by the Cricket.

At the Bugtown Boogie.

Brrrrrrrrrrrrrrrrrrrrrrrrrr.

The Bugtown Boogie.

Shicka. Shicka.

The Bugtown Boogie, shakin' up the woods tonight.

Every kind of bug was there, a-rockin' to the rhythm.

The Katydids had come and brought the Katykids in with 'em.

The Mayfly was a-waltzin' with her little Junebug brother,

As the Caterpillars did the twist, ticklin' each other!

The Beetle grabbed the Butterfly and quickly tried to warn her
Of the Stinkbug who was dancin' by himself there in the corner.
He wasn't really nasty. He was gentle as could be.
But if anyone got near enough for dancin'—phewee!

At the Bugtown Boogie.

Weedle? Weedle?

The Bugtown Boogie.

Chick Chick   Chick Chick.

The Bugtown Boogie, shakin' up the woods tonight.

Well, the crowd was gettin' rowdy, and the band was really jammin'
To the thunder of the drummer playin' Bam! Bam! Bam!
When all at once the music STOPPED . . . and the bugs all turned to see
That standin' sternly on the stairway was *Her Highness, Queen Bee.*

The bugs all stood in silence when they saw the Queen arrive,
Because she never, never ever, nearly never left the hive.
So when she sat down on her throne in front of every bug in town,
They paid attention most politely, 'til she shouted:

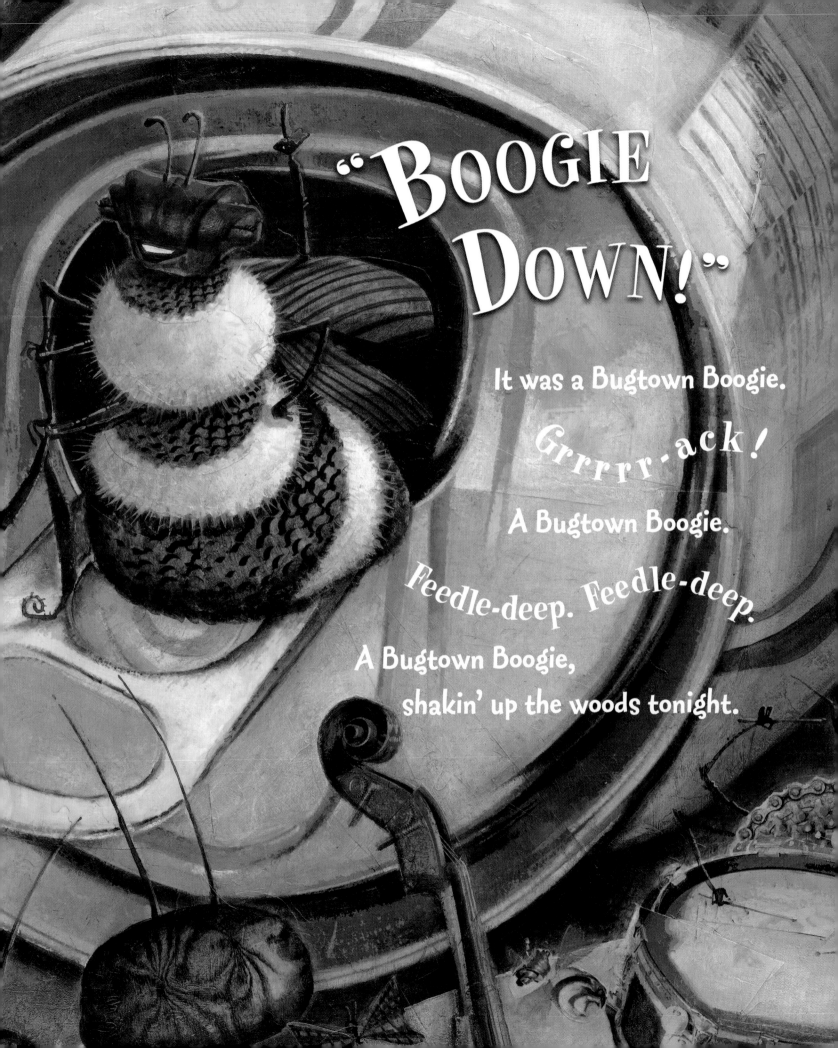

"BOOGIE DOWN!"

It was a Bugtown Boogie.

Grrrrr-ack!

A Bugtown Boogie.

Feedle-deep. Feedle-deep.

A Bugtown Boogie,
shakin' up the woods tonight.

I squatted there a-watchin' 'em and keepin' out of sight,
As they kept right on dancin' through the middle of the night,
While the lights from all the Fireflies and Lightnin' Bugs were flashin'
And the Glowworms were a-glimmerin' in dizzy disco fashion.

Then the sun began to rise, and it took away the moon,
As one by one they wandered homeward to a cozy warm cocoon.
Then someone turned the lights out, and he closed the little door
At the bottom of the tree trunk, where it met the forest floor.

And so I slowly wandered home, as the sun was gettin' bright.
I guess it's time to go to sleep—but I'll be back again tonight!
To watch the Bugtown Boogie.

Wutha wutha. Wutha wutha.

The Bugtown Boogie.

Whrrr. Whrrr.

The Bugtown Boogie, shakin' up the woods tonight.